DAY & NIGHT
IN THE
FOREST

SUSAN and
PETER BARRETT

Illustrated by
PETER BARRETT

D1418211

L HAMMOND World Atlas
Part of the Langenscheidt Publishing Group

HOW TO USE THIS BOOK

1 Read the daytime Introduction on **pages 6–7**

2 Open the flaps on the left- and right-hand sides of the spread to reveal **pages 8–11**, a four-page panoramic foldout of the forest in daytime

3 Read **pages 12–19** to learn all about the daytime animals of the forest that were introduced on pages 8–11

4 Check out **pages 20–21** for a handy guide to the daytime foldout. The simple numbering system will help you identify the many animals you've read about.

5 The nighttime spreads work the same way! Have fun reading!

Daytime

Tree Types
The two main types of trees in the northern forest are conifers (such as fir, spruce, pine), which keep their needle-shaped leaves all year, and deciduous trees (such as oak), which lose their leaves in fall.

Forests cover about 30 percent of Earth's land area. The forests in this book appear in the northern parts of the world. Lying in a band just south of the cold wastelands of the tundra and the snow and ice of the polar regions, these forests provide food and shelter for much wildlife. The trees, plants, mammals, birds, and other animals that live here are similar whether the forest lies in North America, Europe, or northern Asia.

The Northern Forests
The areas colored green on this map show how these forests stretch across the northern regions of the world.

◄ CONIFER FOREST
Conifer forest is composed mainly of tall evergreens, which grow close together. Although little light reaches the forest floor, it does provide food and shelter for a variety of creatures. These include mammals from the deer mouse to the red fox, and birds from woodpeckers to wild turkeys.

Dead Wood, Fungi, Lichens, and Mosses
All of these play an important part in the ecology of the forest. Dead wood is eaten by insect larvae and eventually rots to form earth, helped by the action of fungi. Lichens and mosses cover much of the surface of tree trunks and branches, providing shelter for countless tiny insects and grubs.

DAY & NIGHT
IN THE
FOREST

CONTENTS

DAYTIME

NIGHTTIME

▼ MIXED FOREST

In some places, the forest contains both broad-leaved, deciduous trees and evergreen conifers. Mixed forest like this provides a habitat with a character all its own.

▲ Cones, Leaves, and Seeds

Shown here are branches of spruce and pine with their cones, and oak and maple with their fruit, acorns, and winged seeds. Acorns, and the seeds contained in cones, are spread by animals. They may be either eaten and then left in droppings on the forest floor or buried as food and never dug up. In both cases, the acorns and seeds can take root and eventually grow into trees.

▲ FOREST EDGE

Toward the edges of the forest, the trees thin out. Often there are areas of open ground, providing a different kind of habitat that attracts and supports a variety of wildlife.

◄ Undergrowth, Ferns, and Flowers

In the areas where light can reach the forest floor, bushes, grasses, and flowers grow in soil made rich leaves and bark, fallen and rotted over time. These plants provide food—nectar, berries, and seeds— for a large number of insects, birds, and small mammals.

◄ DENSE FOREST

In some parts of the forest, often in sheltered valleys, the trees grow close together. These areas of dense forest are particularly dark, with little undergrowth.

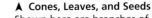

◄ Deer Mouse

Deer mice nest in hollow logs and holes in the ground, where they store nuts and seeds. They are found in many parts of the United States, and their color varies widely.

◄ A deer mouse brings seeds to its store.

▼ Mule Deer

These large deer are not very common in dense forests except in cold weather, when they seek shelter. In fights for females, the males lock antlers, but rarely injure each other badly.

Daytime

Conifer Forest

Dense conifer forests cover enormous areas of land in the northern parts of the world. As conifers never shed all their leaves, the forest floor is dark and little else can grow. However, cones provide seeds for many animals and birds to feed on.

◄ Downy Woodpecker

This woodpecker, the smallest and most common of the forest woodpeckers, is also seen in parks and gardens. The male has a patch of red feathers on the back of his neck.

➤ Hermit Thrush

This brown-spotted bird has perhaps the most beautiful song of all North American birds. Its winter diet of buds and berries is replaced in summer by insects found on the forest floor.

▲ A male hermit thrush singing in the spring

◄ Red Fox

Fox litters usually consist of five or six cubs. The parents bring food to the den while the cubs are small. As the cubs grow, they are brought live prey, and later on they learn to hunt for themselves.

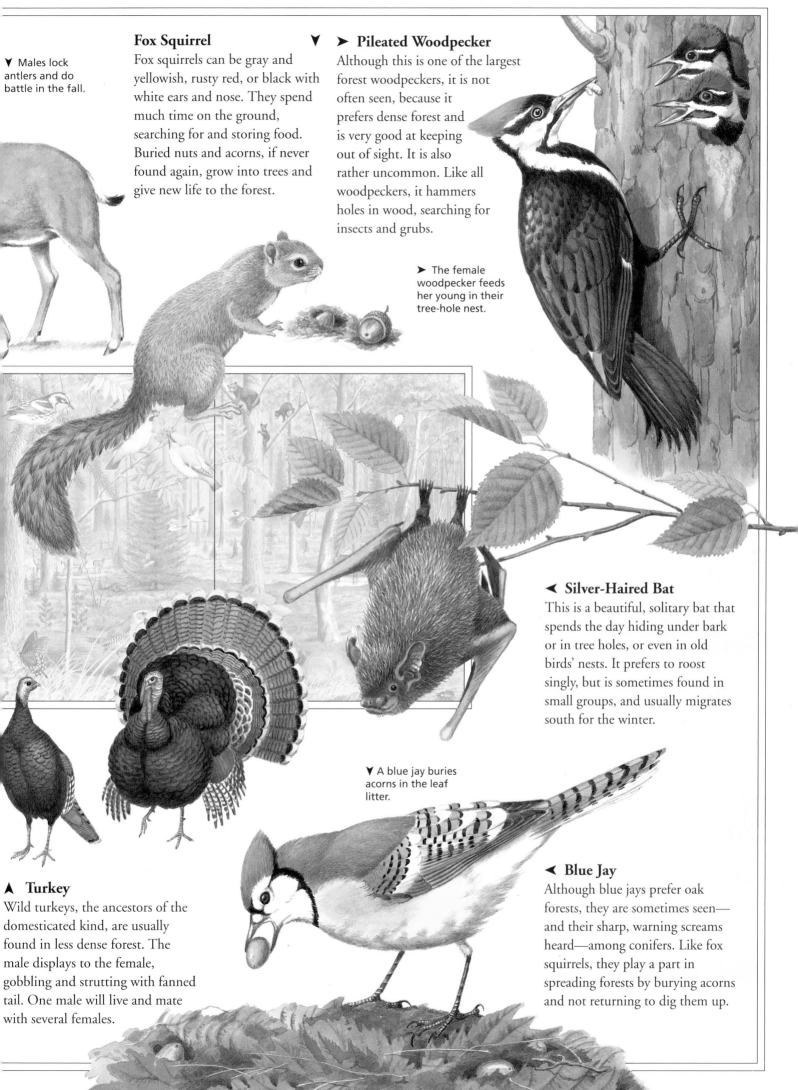

▼ Males lock antlers and do battle in the fall.

Fox Squirrel ▼

Fox squirrels can be gray and yellowish, rusty red, or black with white ears and nose. They spend much time on the ground, searching for and storing food. Buried nuts and acorns, if never found again, grow into trees and give new life to the forest.

➤ Pileated Woodpecker

Although this is one of the largest forest woodpeckers, it is not often seen, because it prefers dense forest and is very good at keeping out of sight. It is also rather uncommon. Like all woodpeckers, it hammers holes in wood, searching for insects and grubs.

➤ The female woodpecker feeds her young in their tree-hole nest.

◄ Silver-Haired Bat

This is a beautiful, solitary bat that spends the day hiding under bark or in tree holes, or even in old birds' nests. It prefers to roost singly, but is sometimes found in small groups, and usually migrates south for the winter.

▼ A blue jay buries acorns in the leaf litter.

▲ Turkey

Wild turkeys, the ancestors of the domesticated kind, are usually found in less dense forest. The male displays to the female, gobbling and strutting with fanned tail. One male will live and mate with several females.

◄ Blue Jay

Although blue jays prefer oak forests, they are sometimes seen—and their sharp, warning screams heard—among conifers. Like fox squirrels, they play a part in spreading forests by burying acorns and not returning to dig them up.

◄ Brown Creeper

This is a shy bird, and is rarely seen, although it can be detected by listening for its soft whistle. It nests on tree trunks, behind peeling pieces of bark, or in tree cracks. Running up trees, it feeds on the insects it finds in the bark.

◄ Eastern Chipmunk

Common in all types of woodland, chipmunks dig burrows in banks where they store seeds and nuts. They carry the food in cheek pouches. Although they can climb well, these squirrels live mainly on the ground.

Daytime
Dense Forest

In some parts of the forest, trees grow close together, forming dense thickets. There may be a mixture of conifer and broadleaf trees, providing a variety of seeds and flowers for the forest animals to eat. Many kinds of birds are found in this part of the forest, and these feed on seeds, nuts, insects, or other birds.

Black Rat Snake ▼

The black rat snake can grow up to nearly 6 feet (2 m) in length. It is a constricting snake, which means it suffocates its victims by coiling around them tightly. Found on farms and other habitats as well as in the forest, it is most active during the day, and feeds mainly on large rodents.

► A black rat snake suffocates a rodent in its coils.

► White-breasted Nuthatch

This is one of the most common American nuthatches. They are short-tailed, acrobatic birds that can climb up, down, and around trees searching for insects. They also eat nuts, which they wedge in cracks and open with blows from their heavy beak.

◄ Saw-whet Owl

Saw-whet owls, roosting in tree holes and dense foliage during the day, can often be approached quite closely. They are named after their call, a raspy sound like a saw being sharpened, heard mainly during the breeding season.

▼ Pine Siskins

These finches feed on the seeds of conifers, alders, and linden. Their nest is a feather-lined saucer of bark and twigs, hidden in the branches of a conifer.

▼ Pine siskins are usually seen in small flocks.

◄ Sharp-shinned Hawk

Sharp-shinned hawks are small and fast-flying, with the rounded wings and long tail of forest hawks. They are expert hunters. They ambush their prey, mainly birds, by suddenly darting out of cover and spearing their victim with their long, sharp claws.

◄ A sharp-shinned hawk catches a blackpoll warbler with its deadly claws.

▲ A bumblebee shown beside its underground nest

▲ Bumblebee

Bumblebees collect nectar from forest flowers. They pollinate flowers and are able to sting just like honeybees. Their nests are quite small. The wax cells contain larvae and pupae, which are looked after by the worker bees.

➤ Butterflies

Butterflies feed off the forest flowers, favoring thistles and knapweed at the forest edge. The illustration shows large, yellow, black-striped tiger swallowtails (above and bottom right) and a silver-bordered fritillary (middle right).

Parula Warbler

This tiny warbler is only about 4 inches (11 cm) long. Living in wet coniferous forests, it lays four or five brown-spotted white eggs in nests built in or behind curtains of Spanish, or beard, moss.

▼

◄ Butterflies feeding on the nectar in flowers

➤ Winter Wren

This tiny wren creeps through the thick vegetation and fallen branches of the forest floor like a mouse. Its domed nest, made of sticks and moss with a side entrance, lies well hidden behind bark, or in tree holes and roots.

➤ Caterpillars

Many caterpillars are found throughout the forest. They provide food for birds, bats, and other small mammals. Some are beautifully camouflaged, while others use intimidating colors or "eye spots" to deter predators.

▼ These waxwings are feasting on juniper berries.

➤ Bohemian Waxwing

These rare visitors to the northern forests feed in large flocks on berries of all kinds. The name comes from shiny, waxlike feathers, which form red spots, like sealing wax, on their wings.

Daytime

Mixed Forest

Where deciduous trees grow among the conifers, the less dense canopy allows more light to reach the forest floor. More flowers grow in these areas. There is a greater variety of seeds and insects, too, which attracts more kinds of birds.

➤ Marten

Martens belong to the weasel family. They make their den in hollow trees and are fierce predators, searching in the treetops for prey such as squirrels. They have sharp claws and a long tail for balance. They also hunt on the ground.

▼ This marten has found a bird's nest and will eat the eggs.

▼ Whip-poor-will

This bird, a type of nightjar, feeds at night. In daytime, it rests on the forest floor, beautifully camouflaged. The chicks are equally well hidden and stay completely still until nightfall, when they are fed.

➤ White-tailed Deer

Born in the early spring, deer fawns can walk at birth, but they remain hidden and completely still, while their mother feeds in the forest. Any movement might give away their position and make them easy prey for foxes, wolves, and bears.

➤ The fawns are camouflaged by their white-spotted coats.

➤ Long-eared Owl

The long-eared owl is strictly nocturnal. But it is so well camouflaged when it roosts during the day, flattening itself against a pine trunk, that it is almost invisible. Although rarely seen, a surprisingly large number of long-eared owls may inhabit an area of forest.

▼ Praying Mantis

Mantises are common in many habitats, including forests. They lie in wait, perfectly still and well camouflaged in low shrubs and grasses. When a victim comes within range, they shoot out their long, spiked forelegs and spear their unsuspecting prey.

▼ Blackburnian Warbler

This warbler nests as high as 80 feet (25 m) above ground. It stays in the upper branches, where it feeds chiefly on insects and berries. In winter, these birds migrate to South America.

A female ▼ warbler feeds her chicks on caterpillars.

▲ Male grouse displaying to female

◀ Spruce Grouse

The male spruce grouse fans his tail like a turkey when he displays to the female. During such displays he also flutters upward and puts up the red combs over his eyes. Spruce grouse are very tame and easy to approach.

◄ Woodland Vole

Voles are small rodents closely related to mice, but more active during the day. The woodland vole spends most of its time in tunnels in the earth and leaf litter. It eats the roots, seeds, leaves, and stems of plants. It also stores food underground to eat at times of shortage.

► Beetles

The grubs of many species of beetle play an important part in turning dead wood into earth. Large larvae bore their way through logs and fallen trees, while smaller ones tunnel just beneath the bark.

◄▼ Purple Finch

Despite their name, the color of the male finch is rosy red, and the female is a streaked dull brown. They feed on seeds and migrate north in spring.

Daytime

Forest Edge

On the edges of the forest, there are fewer conifers. Streams run through groups of alders, birches, and aspens growing on wet ground beside the water. There are many more flowers, which attract butterflies and birds from the open country beyond the forest.

► Beaver

The activities of beavers have important effects on the landscape. With their sharp teeth, they fell small trees for food and to build dams in which they make their homes, called lodges. The dams can be a few hundred yards long. As a result, large ponds are formed and clearings are created in the forest.

▼ Busy beavers at work

Black Bear ►

Bears are more often active at night than in daytime. They will eat almost anything: insects, fruit, leaves, roots, bark, meat, and fish. Being good swimmers, they find it easy to catch all kinds of fish. Salmon is a favorite meal.

➤ Otter

Otters inhabit the lakes and rivers of the woodland edge, rather than the deep forest. They are active by day if not disturbed. The young are born in a riverbank burrow and looked after by their mother for the first eight months of their lives.

◄ An otter burrow entrance can be above or below water level.

◄ Beetle grubs in their tunnels

▲ Cottontail

Cottontails are active day and night. Only in the afternoon do these rabbits rest, hidden in thick brush or a burrow. The babies, nursed by their mother at dawn and dusk, hide quietly in the undergrowth while their mother is out feeding.

➤ Broad-winged Hawk

Broad, rounded wings and a long tail make this hawk an acrobatic flyer, twisting and turning among trees in search of prey. It prefers mice, frogs, and snakes, swooping suddenly on its victims from a hiding place.

◄ A rodent is the next meal for this hawk's chicks.

▲ Moose

Moose are very large deer. The males have enormous, spreading antlers, which are grown in April and shed in the middle of winter. They love to eat plants that grow in streams and lakes, and the water helps to protect them from biting flies. They can be bad tempered and occasionally dangerous.

Caterpillar (36)

Daytime

KEY TO FOLDOUT

Use these numbers if you want to identify any of the animals in the Daytime foldout. Most of the animals are featured on pages 12–19 and are listed here in bold type. Those that are not featured on pages 12–19 are also listed here, together with a brief description.

1 Silver-haired Bat
2 Pileated Woodpecker
3 Mule Deer
4 Downy Woodpecker
5 Red Fox
6 Hermit Thrush
7 Deer Mouse
8 Turkey
9 Fox Squirrel

Beaver (44)

10 Blue Jay

11 Pine Grosbeak
   A large finch, this bird eats mainly berries and buds. The adult males are brightly colored.

12 Pine Siskin
13 Sharp-shinned Hawk
14 Black Rat Snake

◄ White-tailed Deer
When alarmed, the white-tailed deer raises its tail like a flag, warning other deer of the danger. In undisturbed areas, they may be seen in daytime, but they feed mainly at night. By dawn they have usually found a hiding place in thick brush, where they spend the day.

▲ Long-tailed Weasel
Weasels are very fierce predators and can kill prey much larger than themselves. They often stand on their hind legs and peer over the undergrowth on the lookout for food or danger. In the northern part of their range, they turn white in the winter.

▲ Barred Owl
This owl lives in wet forests. It hides during the day in very thick cover, emerging at night to hunt rodents, birds, frogs, and crayfish. It has a distinctive call of loud, rhythmic hoots. The color of its eyes is dark, which is unusual for an owl.

➤ Spring Peeper
This is a tiny frog about 1 inch long when fully grown. It is the most common tree frog in the eastern United States. Its color can vary from gray to brown or green. Its call is loud and musical, and males sing alternating songs in chorus.

➤ Spring peepers are so light they can perch safely on grasses.

➤ Pipistrelle Bat

This tiny bat emerges at dusk to feed on small insects, finding its prey by echolocation. Like all bats, it builds a picture of its surroundings from the echoes of its continual squeaks bouncing back from the objects around it.

➤ Moths

At night, many species of moths come out to feed. Many moths are beautifully camouflaged (above and far right). Some have realistic eye patterns on their hind wings (below right), which can be flashed to frighten off predators. Sphinx moths (below) are very colorful. They feed on the nectar of flowers.

Nighttime

Dense Forest

A t night, moths and bats search for insects, while owls hunt silently for the rodents that have come out to feed. Large animals, such as bears, can be heard rather than seen as they roam the forest on their nighttime excursions looking for food.

➤ These young bears are finding out what's good to eat.

◄ Black Bear

Black bears, whose fur varies in shade from pale brown to black, are more often active at night than by day. They are omnivorous, and eat a variety of foods. Here we see a bear (far left) searching a rotted tree stump for grubs, while another bear feasts on the red berries of a mountain ash.

◄ Silver-haired Bat
The black hairs of this bat are tipped with silver, giving it a frosted appearance. It appears early in the evening and can often be seen along the banks of streams and rivers. It feeds on insects, especially moths and flies.

▲ Red Fox
The red fox has extremely good hearing, which helps it to hunt in the nighttime darkness of the conifer forests. It catches rodents by listening carefully, jumping high into the air, and pouncing on its prey with its forefeet.

Nighttime

Conifer Forest

The conifer forest at night is dark and silent except for the cries of hunting owls. Animals that have hidden all day in the shelter of the leaves, or in holes in branches or roots, emerge to search for food under cover of darkness.

▼ The mother skunk takes her family of young everywhere with her during the early part of their lives. They learn from her what is good to eat.

Striped Skunk ➤
The bold black-and-white stripes of this skunk carry the warning "Do not disturb." When annoyed, the skunk snarls loudly and stands on its forefeet, as though doing a handstand. In an emergency, it can spray its enemy with a jet of foul-smelling liquid from under its tail. The smell is very strong and long-lasting.

◄ MIXED FOREST

The mix of animals active at night in these areas is largely different from that during the daytime, but the forest is just as alive with movement and sound.

▼ Seeing in the Dark

Many nocturnal mammals and birds have eyes with special features that help them see in the dark. A common feature is the way the pupil, the central dark part of the eye, grows larger the less light there is. You can see the change in the eyes of the lynx (below). During the day, the pupil is a small slit, but at night it fills almost the entire eye.

Daytime   *Nighttime*

▼ FOREST EDGE

At the forest edge, the trees are fewer and farther between. Some light—from the moon—shines through the canopy even at night.

▲ Echolocation

Bats use echolocation for pinpointing objects or prey in the dark. They do this by sending out a series of high-pitched squeaks and picking up the echo of anything in their path.

◄ Tree Homes

Forest creatures find all kinds of places to shelter, nest, and live in. There are holes made in tree trunks by woodpeckers.

Other holes can be dug out of rotting branches and fallen logs. Some small animals make their homes in the twisted roots of trees.

15 **Eastern Chipmunk**

16 **Bumblebee**

17 **Silver-bordered Fritillary**

18 **Tiger Swallowtail**

19 **Parula Warbler**

20 **Brown Creeper**

21 **White-Breasted Nuthatch**

22 **Saw-whet Owl**

23 **Long-eared Owl**

27 Eastern-tailed Blue
One of several hundred kinds of small butterflies noted for their brilliant blue color

28 **Praying Mantis**

29 **Winter Wren**

30 **Whip-poor-will**

31 **Spruce Grouse**

32 **Marten**

35 **Bohemian Waxwing**

36 **Caterpillar**

37 **Black Bear**

38 Raccoon
This animal spends the day sleeping in places such as hollow logs (see page 32).

39 **Woodland Vole**

40 **Cottontail**

Silver-haired Bat (1)

24 **Blackburnian Warbler**

25 **White-tailed Deer**

26 Spicebrush Swallowtail
There are several hundred different kinds of swallowtail butterfly. They may be very attractive and are often quite large.

33 Spring Azure
Another example of a blue butterfly that inhabits the northern forests.

34 Boreal Chickadee
Distinguished by its brown head, this bird belongs to the titmouse family and is one of seven kinds of chickadee. They usually nest in holes in tree trunks.

41 **Moose**

42 **Purple Finch**

43 **Broad-winged Hawk**

44 **Beaver**

45 **Otter**

46 **Beetle**

Broad-winged Hawk (43)

Nighttime

During the night, the forest is a dark and mysterious place. But it is not deserted. Many animals and birds, which might spend the day hidden in holes in tree trunks, among roots, or in dense thickets, come out at night to hunt and feed. Bats and owls fly without a sound through the trees, and moths feed on the sweet sap of tree trunks and the nectar of flowers.

▲ Day and Night Pollination
Flowers need to be pollinated to form fruit. Birds play a large role in this, gathering and shedding pollen accidentally as they search for insects. Moths and other insects feed on pollen and nectar during the night.

▲ Hunting in the Dark
Owls have excellent night vision, but rely mainly on their hearing to locate prey. Disks of fine feathers funnel sound into their ears.

▲ CONIFER FOREST
Fewer shrubs and flowers grow among conifers, as little light reaches the forest floor through the thick tree cover.

◄ DENSE FOREST
The dense forest is particularly dark at night. The way the trees grow thickly together makes hunting difficult for predators.

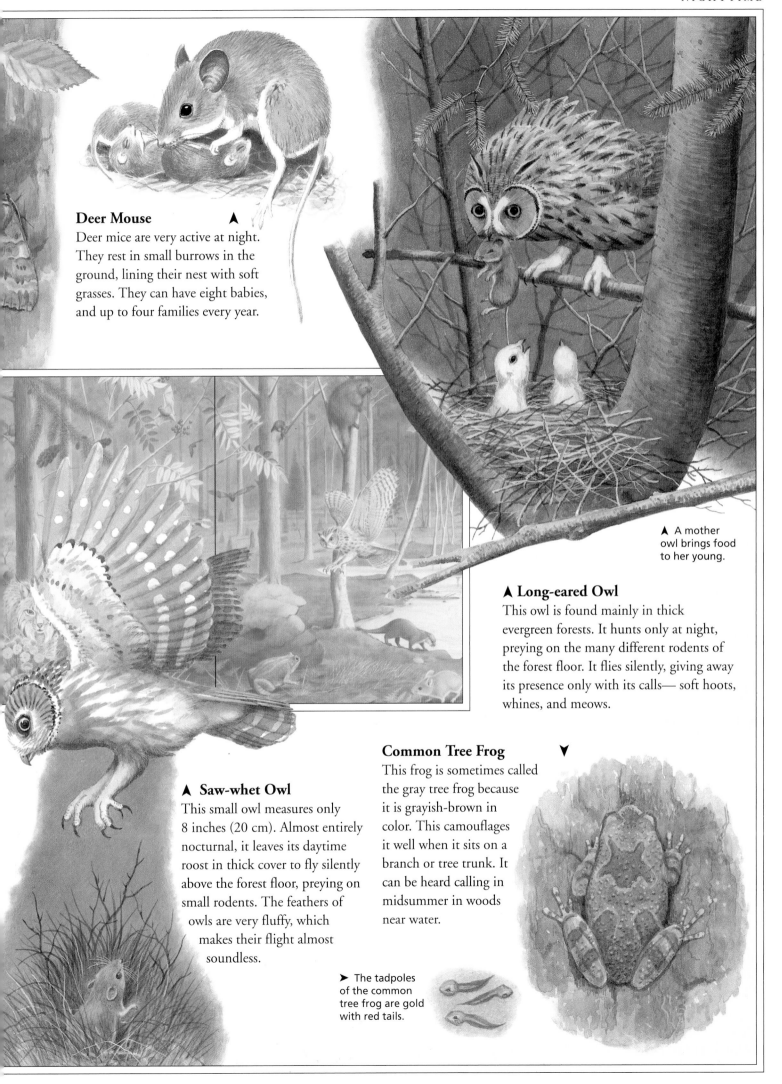

Deer Mouse ▲

Deer mice are very active at night. They rest in small burrows in the ground, lining their nest with soft grasses. They can have eight babies, and up to four families every year.

▲ A mother owl brings food to her young.

▲ Long-eared Owl

This owl is found mainly in thick evergreen forests. It hunts only at night, preying on the many different rodents of the forest floor. It flies silently, giving away its presence only with its calls— soft hoots, whines, and meows.

▲ Saw-whet Owl

This small owl measures only 8 inches (20 cm). Almost entirely nocturnal, it leaves its daytime roost in thick cover to fly silently above the forest floor, preying on small rodents. The feathers of owls are very fluffy, which makes their flight almost soundless.

Common Tree Frog ▼

This frog is sometimes called the gray tree frog because it is grayish-brown in color. This camouflages it well when it sits on a branch or tree trunk. It can be heard calling in midsummer in woods near water.

► The tadpoles of the common tree frog are gold with red tails.

➤ Underwing Moths

These moths rest camouflaged in vegetation during the day. At night, they feed on nectar and the sap of trees. Many, such as the yellow underwing moth (right), have brightly colored hind wings that flash in flight, confusing an attacker, and making this moth hard to catch. Underwings also have a special hearing organ that can pick up the high-pitched sounds made by bats, which they evade by flying in irregular patterns.

➤ Little Brown Myotis

This bat is about to use its tail membrane to catch a moth. Myotis bats spend summertime days in old buildings or trees, hibernating in caves during the winter.

▼ This little brown myotis has caught a moth, which it is about to eat.

Nighttime

Mixed Forest

The calls of owls and nightjars break the silence of the forest at night, and the howls of coyotes and wolves echo through the trees. The forest is full of hunting bats, especially at dusk, but their high-pitched squeaking cannot normally be heard by humans.

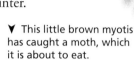

➤ A raccoon searches for food at the edge of a stream.

◄ Raccoon

Raccoons are mostly nocturnal and solitary, spending the day asleep in tree holes or hollow logs. They use water to improve the sense of touch in their paws, not to wash food as was sometimes thought in the past. They hunt in streams, turning over stones to find crayfish, fish, or turtles.

▲ Whip-poor-will

When these nightjars emerge to feed at night, they may be seen flying silently in search of insects. Their beaks, which open very wide, are lined with stiff hairs, forming a sort of net that traps insects in their mouths.

▼ Coyote

At dusk, as they gather to hunt, coyotes call to each other, making a chorus of howls. They maintain contact calls throughout the night. Coyotes, members of the dog family, are like small wolves, though they tend not to form large packs. They eat almost anything, including rotting animal flesh, and even large prey, such as deer.

▼ Turkey

During the hours of darkness, turkeys roost in trees, often over water for added protection. They are the largest American game bird, reaching a length of 48 inches (120 cm). During the day, they feed in small groups, finding seeds and insects on the forest floor.

▼ Sphinx Moths

There are many species of sphinx moth. They are usually large and often have brightly colored hind wings. They feed by hovering like hummingbirds in front of plants, flicking their very long tongues into flower blossom in search of nectar.

◄ Lynx

The lynx is generally an animal of colder, more northerly and barren areas, but it also lives in forests. It is a powerful cat and preys chiefly on hares and rabbits. It usually rests during the day, hunting mostly at night.

➤ These sphinx moths are feeding at sunset on trumpet flowers.

◄ Spadefoot Toad
The skin of spadefoot toads is smoother than the warty skin of garden toads. They have hard, horny pads on their large hind feet. These growths, which give them their name, help them dig underground burrows, where they may stay for months. The pupils of their eyes, like those of cats, grow round in the dark. Spadefoot toads are generally classified as frogs.

Nighttime

Forest Edge

As night falls, many creatures come out of their hiding places. Some, like mice, frogs, and toads, are rarely seen in daytime. Animals from the edge of the forest make their way into the trees, looking for food and shelter.

► This porcupine is ready to attack an inquisitive raccoon.

▲ White-footed Mouse
Mice are the most common mammals in the forest. They are active day and night, all year round. They feed on seeds, nuts, fruit, and insects, and are preyed on by many of the larger forest animals and birds.

► Porcupine
The porcupine is primarily nocturnal and solitary. An excellent climber, it feeds among the forest trees on leaves, twigs, and bark. If disturbed and forced to fight, it puts up its sharp quills and backs tail first toward the enemy. The quills are barbed and very hard to get out.

◄ A marten chases a fox squirrel along a pine branch.

◄ Marten

Martens are active by day and night, hunting in the branches of the trees for their prey. They hunt for squirrels and birds in the treetops and can catch fleeing squirrels with ease. They also eat birds' eggs, rabbits, mice, and even fruit and nuts.

▼ Great Horned Owl

When threatened, this large owl crouches down on a branch, spreads its wings, and puffs itself up to look as frightening as possible. It is a fearsome hunter, swooping down so fast and silently that its prey has almost no chance of escape.

▲ Hoary Bat

This large bat hangs hidden in the branches of evergreen trees during the day. It comes out late in the evening and is usually solitary and rarely seen. It mostly eats moths. Hoary bats migrate south in winter.

► Otter

Otters hunt by night as well as during the day. They are marvelous swimmers and can remain underwater for several minutes. They catch all sorts of fish with ease but are particularly fond of eels, which they may carry to the riverbank to eat.

Nighttime

KEY TO FOLDOUT

Use these numbers if you want to identify
any of the animals on the Nighttime foldout.
Except for the Swift Moth, they are all
featured on pages 28–35.

Little Brown Myotis (24)

Raccoon (21)

Common Tree Frog (12)

1 Silver-haired Bat

2 White-tailed Deer

3 Striped Skunk

4 Long-tailed Weasel

5 Spring Peeper

6 Red Fox

7 Barred Owl

8 Pipistrelle Bat

16 Saw-whet Owl

17 Turkey

18 Lynx

19 Red Underwing Moth

20 Sphinx Moth

21 Raccoon

22 Coyote

23 Whip-poor-will

Sphinx Moths (20)

9 Long-eared Owl

10 Black Bear

11 Deer Mouse

12 Common Tree Frog

13 Sphinx Moth

14 Yellow Underwing Moth

15 Swift Moth
   Swift moth larvae live
   underground and feed on roots.

24 Little Brown Myotis

25 Marten

26 Spadefoot Toad

27 Great Horned Owl

28 Porcupine

29 Hoary Bat

30 Otter

31 White-footed Mouse

Turkey (17)

GLOSSARY

brush dense undergrowth of bushes and shrubs

camouflage an animal's natural coloring that allows it to blend in with its surroundings

canopy the layer of leaves and branches formed by the treetops, which covers the ground below

domesticated an animal that has been adapted to live in a human environment instead of in the wild

ecology the study of the relationship between plants, animals, and their environment

habitat the place and conditions in which a plant or animal lives

larva (plural **larvae**) the newly hatched, grublike form of an insect

migrate to move from one region to another according to the seasons

nocturnal sleeping during the day and being active at night

omnivorous eating all types of food: meat, fish, plants, eggs, etc.

predator an animal that hunts other animals for food

pupa (plural **pupae**) the stage of an insect's development between a larva and an adult

roost to rest or sleep; or a place to rest or sleep

solitary spending a lot of time alone

tundra a cold, dry, treeless area, close to the North Pole, with few plants and animals

INDEX